Hudson an Playing

for Marcus and Caspar 🐾

This is me.

This is Hudson.

Hudson is my new puppy and my best friend.

We love playing together
all day long.

I like running.

Hudson likes running!

I like jumping.

Hudson likes jumping!

I like rolling.

Hudson likes rolling!

I like climbing.

Hudson likes climbing!

so he is not very good at this!

I like digging.

Hudson likes digging!

I like dancing.

Hudson likes dancing!

pheweee!

Life is very busy...

But at the end of the day
we both like.....

I love Hudson.

And he loves me.

The End

Collect all 5 books in the
'Hudson and Me' series!

Available to buy at Amazon:
www.amazon.co.uk/com/eu

Hudson and Me
Hudson and Me Playing
Hudson and Me Snacktime
Hudson and Me Exploring
Hudson and Me Bedtime

Visit Hudson's website to see all the books, learn about Hudson,
and download activities for your little ones:

www.hudsonandme.co.uk

Printed in Great Britain
by Amazon